CONFLICTS, CHANGES, AND CONFEDERATION
1770-1867

TITLE LIST

CONFLICTS, CHANGES, AND CONFEDERATION
1770-1867

BY
SHEILA NELSON

MASON CREST PUBLISHERS
PHILADELPHIA

Mason Crest Publishers Inc.
370 Reed Road
Broomall, Pennsylvania 19008
(866) MCP-BOOK (toll free)

First printing
1 2 3 4 5 6 7 8 9 10

Library of Congress Cataloging-in-Publication Data

Nelson, Sheila.
  Conflicts, changes, and confederation, 1770–1867 / by Sheila Nelson.
      p. cm. — (How Canada became Canada)
  Includes index.
  ISBN 1-4222-0004-3   ISBN 1-4222-0000-0 (series)
  1. Canada—History—1763–1867—Juvenile literature. I. Title.
  F1032.N45 2006
  971.03—dc22
                          2005007153

Produced by Harding House Publishing Service, Inc.
www.hardinghousepages.com
Interior design by MK Bassett-Harvey.
Cover design by Dianne Hodack.
Printed in the Hashemite Kingdom of Jordan.

CONTENTS

INTRODUCTION

by David Bercuson

Every country's history is distinct, and so is Canada's. Although Canada is often said to be a pale imitation of the United States, it has a unique history that has created a modern North American nation on its own path to democracy and social justice. This series explains how that happened.

Canada's history is rooted in its climate, its geography, and in its separate political development. Virtually all of Canada experiences long, dark, and very cold winters with copious amounts of snowfall. Canada also spans several distinct geographic regions, from the rugged western mountain ranges on the Pacific coast to the forested lowlands of the St. Lawrence River Valley and the Atlantic tidewater region.

Canada's regional divisions were complicated by the British conquest of New France at the end of the Seven Years' War in 1763. Although Britain defeated France, the French were far more numerous in Canada than the British. Britain was thus forced to recognize French Canadian rights to their own language, religion, and culture. That recognition is now enshrined in the Canadian Constitution. It has made Canada a democracy that values group rights alongside individual rights, with official French/English bilingualism as a key part of the Canadian character.

During the American Revolution, Canadians chose to stay British. After the Revolution, they provided refuge to tens of thousands of Americans who, for one reason or another, did not follow George Washington, Benjamin Franklin, or the other founders of the United States who broke with Britain.

Democracy in Canada under the British Crown evolved more slowly than it did in the United States. But in the early nineteenth century, slavery was outlawed in the

British Empire, and as a result, also in Canada. Thus Canada never experienced civil war or government-imposed racial segregation.

From these few, brief examples, it is clear that Canada's history differs considerably from that of the United States. And yet today, Canada is a true North American democracy in its own right. Canadians will profit from a better understanding of how their country was shaped—and Americans may learn much about their own country by studying the story of Canada.

One

THE AMERICAN COLONIES REVOLT

Nobody was happy. The French and Indian Wars had ended, and Britain ruled North America—but the colonies began to find they did not like being restricted by laws made in Britain. The Royal Proclamation of 1763 had forbidden settlement west of the Appalachian Mountains, allowing colonists to live only along a narrow strip of land several hundred miles wide along the East Coast. Settlers from the American colonies who already lived west of the line were not pleased with the proclamation. Québec and the settlements along the St. Lawrence River had not been included in the restricted zone, but the Canadians in the newly created province of Québec were unhappy as well.

The British had conquered Québec in 1763, and almost all its inhabitants were French. The proclamation imposed British law on the province, hoping to attract British settlers to the area. French laws would no longer govern the French Canadians living there. Worse, British law said Roman Catholics could not hold government offices—and almost all the Canadians were Roman Catholics.

James Murray, Québec's British governor, refused to enforce many of the new laws and instead worked with the French, letting them keep their own civil laws. The British merchants who had moved to Québec after 1763 complained in London about Murray's

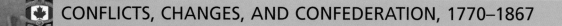

attitude. They had expected—and wanted—to be governed by the British laws, and they also expected to be a part of a new governing assembly in the province. Murray refused to call a meeting of the assembly, knowing the French could not take part because they were Catholics.

Soon, Murray was recalled to Britain to face an inquiry into his leadership of Québec, and Guy Carleton replaced him as governor. Carleton, like Murray, believed Québec should be governed with a blend of French and British laws and customs. He did not think many British settlers would want to live in Québec anyway, since the weather was much harsher than in the southern colonies. He believed the British government should accept the presence of the French and learn to work with them instead of trying to transform them into English-speaking Protestants.

The Quebec Act

Carleton's opinions on Québec finally convinced the leaders in London, and in 1774, Britain passed the Quebec Act. The act extended the borders of Québec south to include the area between the Ohio and Mississippi rivers, where many French settlers lived. The act also said Québec would be ruled by British criminal law but by

Quebec City's Citadel

Criminal Law and Civil Law: What's the Difference?

Criminal law involves a citizen and the state or federal government acting on behalf of the "wronged." Criminal law cases are characterized by the need to investigate crimes, prosecute defendants, and hold convicted defendants accountable, usually through incarceration. The district attorney usually represents the state, and defendants must be found guilty beyond a reasonable doubt.

Civil law deals with cases in which people have been harmed and a financial award might help the situation. Private attorneys generally represent the parties involved, and the usual punishment involves payment of money damages or a fine. Rarely is a prison sentence given. In civil cases, the burden of guilt is much less than in criminal cases. A defendant in a civil case needs only to be found guilty by a preponderance of evidence.

ANNO DECIMO QUARTO

Georgii III. Regis.

CAP. LXXXVIII.

An Act to establish a Fund towards further defraying the Charges of the Administration of Justice, and Support of the Civil Government within the Province of *Quebec*, in *America*.

WHEREAS certain Duties were imposed, by the Authority of His most Christian Majesty, upon Wine, Rum, Brandy, Eau de Vie de Liqueur, imported into the Province of Canada, now called the Province of Quebec, and also a Duty of Three Pounds per Centum ad Valorem, upon all dry Goods imported into, and exported from, the said Province, which Duties subsisted at the Time of the Surrender of the said Province to Your Majesty's Forces in the late War: And whereas it is expedient that the said Duties should cease and be discontinued; and that in Lieu and in Stead thereof, other Duties should be raised by the Authority of Parliament, for making a more adequate Provision for defraying the Charge of the

*Preamble.
Certain Duties imposed by His most Christian Majesty upon Rum, Brandy, etc. imported into Quebec,*

21 P 2

7

A copy of the Quebec Act

French civil law and allowed Roman Catholics to hold public offices. In this way, the French would be allowed to participate in governing their own region.

American colonists were furious when they heard about the Quebec Act. They had been involved in an increasing power struggle with British Parliament, and they worried about Britain giving too much power to Roman Catholics. Many of the colonists had left Europe to find religious freedom or to escape conflicts over religion. They did not want the same clashes to happen in their new land.

British Parliament was aware of the growing dissatisfaction in their American colonies, but they worried too about the French-speaking Canadians they now ruled. The governors of Québec, James Murray and Guy Carleton, recommended finding a compromise of British and French laws to keep the Canadians from rebelling. The Quebec Act was intended to provide just that compromise.

The Quebec Act more or less satisfied the Canadians, but the American colonists considered it one of the Intolerable Acts. These were a list of laws passed by British Parliament that outraged the Americans. Many of the Intolerable Acts involved taxing the colonists without giving them the power to represent their own interests in Parliament. The Quebec Act, however, empowered the French Canadians—the colonists' enemies through nearly one hundred years of bloody warfare—with territory and rights the Americans did not believe the French Canadians should have.

England's Parliament buildings

13

The Continental Congress

The Continental Congress

In 1775, the American colonists held the Second Continental Congress to discuss how they would deal with their complaints against the British Parliament. They sent a letter inviting the Canadians to send delegates to the Congress, expecting they would want to join with them against Britain. Many of the English-speaking Canadians had come from the American colonies not long before, and the French obviously had reasons to hate the British.

The Americans waited expectantly for the Canadian delegates to arrive, but none came. Many of the English merchants who

14

An Invitation

The Continental Congress sent the following letter to the Canadians, asking them to join in the fight against Britain. As the war continued, the Congress continued to send letters urging the Canadians to become the fourteenth colony in the United States of America.

To the oppressed Inhabitants of Canada.

Friends and countrymen,

. . . Since the conclusion of the late war, we have been happy in considering you as fellow-subjects, and from the commencement of the present plan for subjugating the continent, we have viewed you as fellow-sufferers with us. . . .

We are informed you have already been called upon to waste your lives in a contest with us. Should you, by complying in this instance, assent to your new establishment, and a war break out with France, your wealth and your sons may be sent to perish in expeditions against their islands in the West Indies.

It cannot be presumed that these considerations will have no weight with you, or that you are so lost to all sense of honor. We can never believe that the present race of Canadians are so degenerated as to possess neither the spirit, the gallantry, nor the courage of their ancestors. You certainly will not permit the infamy and disgrace of such pusillanimity to rest on your own heads, and the consequences of it on your children forever.

. . . As our concern for your welfare entitles us to your friendship, we presume you will not, by doing us injury, reduce us to the disagreeable necessity of treating you as enemies. . . .

had moved to Québec were enjoying the extra territory the Quebec Act had given them, and they were not angry enough at Britain to care about the Continental Congress. The French did not want to get involved. They had recently been at war with the American colonies, and they saw no reason to trust them now.

The Invasion

The American response to the Canadian lack of enthusiasm for their cause was to launch an attack against Québec in September of 1775. They feared the British would use Canada as a base from which to send out attacks, and they wanted to strike quickly be-

The War and the Canadian Atlantic Colonies

The American Revolution most directly affected the province of Québec, but the colony of Nova Scotia and the fishing settlements of Newfoundland were also impacted by the war to their south. Both Nova Scotia and Newfoundland lost all their trade with the American colonies, while Nova Scotia faced the threat of invasion from the American colonies. The Americans wanted Nova Scotia to join them in breaking away from British control, but most Nova Scotians were not interested, even though many of them originally came from New England. For one thing, the British military was centered in Halifax, which discouraged thoughts of an uprising. For another, the population was scattered and difficult to unite in rebellion. Most of all, however, Nova Scotia had just experienced a major religious revival, and the people strongly desired peace.

fore Britain fortified the northern colonies extensively. They also believed the Canadians really wanted to be freed from the British, in spite of what they claimed.

Two groups set out to capture the two main cities in Canada: Montréal and Québec City. Richard Montgomery would lead 1,500 men to attack Montréal, while at the same time, Benedict Arnold would travel north to Québec City with 1,200 men.

*A **siege** is a military operation in which an army surrounds a place and cuts it off from all outside access until it is forced to surrender.*

Defeats and Victories

Montgomery laid *siege* to Montréal, where Governor Carleton lived. Nearly two months later, in early November, the Americans finally succeeded in capturing the city. Carleton escaped the day before Montgomery broke into the city and fled to Québec City.

Because of the difficult terrain, the Americans took much longer to reach Québec City than they had Montréal, which they had approached along the St. Lawrence River. Arnold finally reached the city on December 3, but by then half his men had died or deserted. The Americans were hungry and tired, but they confidently expected the people of the countryside to rise up and join them in the fight against British oppression. Governor Carleton, for his part, expected the French Canadians to help fight on the side of the British to drive off the Americans. The French Canadians did neither, choosing to stay neutral, to the dismay of both sides.

The Americans set up camp outside Québec City, but the generals, Montgomery and Arnold, could not afford to wait for a siege to wear down the Canadians. Winter had arrived, and the American troops were cold and hungry. The French

Benedict Arnold

Richard Montgomery

in the leg. Despite the loss of their leaders, the men fought on for hours, breaking through a barricade and wandering through the streets in a blur of whirling snow. When officers finally tried to call a retreat, the Americans found the British had blocked their way out of the city.

The battle deteriorated further, with British soldiers firing down from housetops at the American troops in the streets below. Eventually, all the American soldiers in the city had been either killed or captured as they got lost in the maze of streets and were separated from each other. Sixty Americans were killed and over four hundred captured in the battle; the British lost only five men.

General Arnold had evaded capture, since he had retreated earlier after being shot. He and the remaining six hundred American soldiers pulled back from the city and set up camp about a mile away to wait for reinforcements. Arnold refused to give up right away on the campaign that had cost him so much.

The Americans had gone into Canada expecting to raise an army when they arrived. They found the French Canadian farmers were not as interested in joining them as they had assumed. At first, the Americans bought food and supplies from the Canadians, but they expected to pay for it with the paper money the Continental

Canadian farmers sold them supplies—as they sold supplies to the British in the city— but they had not joined them in fighting. Many American soldiers wanted to go home. Their contracts expired at the end of the year, and the generals feared they would all leave before the city had been conquered.

On December 31, 1775, under cover of a blizzard, the Americans attacked Québec City. General Montgomery was killed in the initial attack, and General Arnold was shot

Death of General Montgomery

*If an action is **concentrated**, it is focused on a particular purpose or activity.*

Congress had printed. The Canadians did not want paper money, which they considered worthless pieces of paper; they wanted hard currency—in other words, coins. When the Canadians realized the Americans could not pay, they stopped helping them at all. As a result, the Americans started raiding farms to get the supplies they needed. This practice did not make them better liked.

In 1783, the American Revolutionary War ended with the Treaty of Paris, but the war in Canada was over long before that. Although the Continental Congress continued to hold out hope that the Canadians would join them, they made no more **concentrated** attacks on Canadian targets. At the end of

A copy of the Treaty of Paris

Paper money printed by the Continental Congress

The Revolution and the Iroquois Confederacy

When the Revolutionary War broke out, the Iroquois Confederacy—made up of the Mohawk, Oneida, Onondaga, Cayuga, Seneca, and Tuscarora tribes—chose to let each tribe decide on its own whether to support the British or the Americans. This decision tore the Confederacy apart since all the tribes except the Oneida supported the British. After the war, some chose to make peace with the Americans, but others, such as Joseph Brant, a Mohawk chief, settled permanently in Canada.

the war, when the French once again suggested "freeing" Canada, the Congress agreed this was a good idea but said they could not afford to send troops. For the time being, Canada was left alone.

Although they had resisted being drawn into the American fight for freedom, the Canadians were not unaffected by the war. When it was clear the Americans would be victorious, thousands of Loyalists—those faithful to Britain and King George—fled into Canada to begin new lives. This flood of people would change the face of Canada forever.

Two
THE LOYALISTS MOVE NORTH

The city noises faded first, and then the familiar New York City skyline began to disappear as the ships left the harbor. Many of the people had tears in their eyes or on their cheeks as they stood at the railings watching all that they knew slip into the distance. The city was no longer their home, not since the war ended with the British defeat.

The Evacuation

On November 25, 1783, the British officially left New York City, and George Washington marched into the city in triumph. With the troops went thousands of Loyalist families. Many had already fled north to Canada during the war, in wagons or boats. Thirty thousand streamed out of New York City alone at the end of the war. In all, nearly one hundred thousand Loyalists left the new United States of America. Some went back to Britain, some traveled to the Bahamas, and half went to Canada.

Though some of these refugees were the rich aristocrats who believed in the British monarchy, many were ordinary people—farmers, tradespeople, and clergy. Some were not even British, but immigrants from throughout Europe; Britain had given them the chance to begin new lives in the American colonies.

For all of them, leaving the American colonies meant giving up their homes and beginning new lives, but for some the changes were more drastic than for others. Many had lived in large, established cities such as Boston, New York, or Philadelphia.

As they arrived in Nova Scotia and saw the wilderness of forests and untamed land before them, many cried again at their loss.

Loyalist immigrants quickly swamped the city of Halifax. People camped in churches or in the streets. The town of Shelburne sprang up at the southern tip of Nova Scotia, although the land was not suitable for farming and most of the people who settled there moved on after two or three years.

Loyalist families traveled up the St. John River and rebuilt a deserted French settlement into the town of Fredericton. Thousands arrived in Québec, but the governor, fearing they would clash with the French, encouraged them to move further west along the St. Lawrence River and the northern shore of Lake Ontario.

The British government wanted to compensate the Loyalists for the land and property they had lost in the American Revolutionary War. They agreed to give land to anyone who wanted it—all they had to do was promise to be loyal to the British king. Some Americans, hearing about the free land, went north as well and settled in the new Loyalist towns.

With the arrival of the Loyalists, the population of Canada nearly doubled. New areas were settled, towns founded,

Halifax in the 1780s

and roads built. Now, for the first time, the Canadian population included a significant number of English-speaking people. The Loyalists valued stability and were generally very *conservative*. These were some of the reasons they had not joined with the rebels during the Revolutionary War.

*If someone is **conservative**, he or she is reluctant to accept abrupt change and prefers to keep things the way they are.*

The Need for New Colonies

Before the American Revolution had led to the arrival of tens of thousands of Loyalists, Canada had consisted of three provinces—Québec, Nova Scotia, and tiny Prince Edward Island. The island of Newfoundland was not officially recognized as a colony at this time. A lieutenant-governor ruled each province, with one governor overseeing the whole of Canada.

With so many new arrivals, the lieutenant-governor of Nova Scotia found it increasingly difficult to deal

A Population Explosion

Estimates for the population of Canada:

1765—69,810

1784—113,012

1790—161,311

with the needs of the population. New towns had grown up almost overnight, scattered across remote wilderness areas.

To manage the greater population, Nova Scotia was divided into three colonies in 1784—Cape Breton Island, Nova Scotia, and New Brunswick. (In 1820, Cape Breton Island would rejoin Nova Scotia.) Before the Loyalists moved north to Canada, New Brunswick had been sparsely populated, with only a few communities along the Bay of Fundy and some Acadian settlements on the Gulf of St. Lawrence. Within only twenty years, New Brunswick's population had risen to about thirty-five thousand.

Splitting Québec

The English-speaking Loyalists who had settled in the province of Québec were tired of being ruled by French laws. In 1774, the

The Black Loyalists

When the Loyalists fled north to Canada, over three thousand free blacks went with them. Many of these were former slaves who had escaped from their masters during the war. When Americans tried to reclaim their slaves, the British refused and instead granted the blacks their freedom. Although the blacks were now free, they still faced the prejudices of their white neighbors. The Black Loyalists settled in small, poor communities and worked at the most difficult jobs, such as clearing brush and building houses for those immigrants who were not used to manual labor. In 1792, about 1,200 of these Black Loyalists left Nova Scotia and traveled to Africa, where they founded Sierra Leone.

Quebec Act had set up a blend of French and British laws and practices. This blend had worked at the time, since most of the residents had been French, but with more English-speaking colonists arriving all the time, some change was needed. Nova Scotia had already been divided into three parts due to the huge numbers of Loyalist immigrants. Most thought a similar division was needed in Québec.

In 1791, the Constitutional Act split the province of Québec into two parts—Upper Canada and Lower Canada. Lower Canada (which would later become Québec) would keep its blend of French and British laws and would be mainly French-speaking. Upper Canada, in the newly settled Lake Ontario region, would be English-speaking and would not be ruled by French laws.

The Constitutional Act also introduced a new form of government in Canada. Each province would still have a lieutenant-governor, who answered to a central governor of Canada. Under each provincial governor was an appointed council. Under the council was the assembly, an elected group of

Yonge Street

In 1796, Toronto's Yonge Street was built. It is acknowledged as the longest street in the world—1,190 miles (1,900 kilometers).

Loyalists nearly doubled Canada's population in the 1780s.

27

landowning men. The major change was the council, the appointed group. British Parliament believed the American colonies had rebelled because they had too much freedom to govern themselves; they wanted to make sure the same thing did not happen in Canada. The elected assembly gave the people a voice in their own government, but the assembly could do nothing without the approval of the council and the lieutenant-governor.

John Graves Simcoe

John Graves Simcoe was the first lieutenant-governor of Upper Canada. Simcoe had great hopes for the new province. He wanted to turn Upper Canada into the ideal British colony.

In 1793, Simcoe began to build the new capital of Upper Canada at York (now Toronto) on Lake Ontario. He had originally held government meetings at Newark (later called Niagara-on-the-Lake), but he felt the location was too close to the U.S. border to be safe from possible attacks. His original choice for the new capital was a site he named London, but the governor rejected the spot because it was too remote.

Simcoe invited Americans to settle in the new province and offered them land at no

John Graves Simcoe

cost. All they needed to do was swear their loyalty to Britain. Many took him up on his offer, and the population of Upper Canada continued to grow.

During his short term as lieutenant-governor, Simcoe built towns and roads, set up a court system, and introduced trials by jury. Most important, he outlawed slavery. Simcoe had always hated slavery, so when Peter Martin, a leader in the free black community of Upper Canada, petitioned for a ban on slavery, Simcoe agreed without hesitation. Many Loyalist families in the province had brought their slaves with them from the American colonies when they moved north after the war. These slave owners were alarmed when they heard about Simcoe's proposed slavery ban and tried their best to stop the law. Simcoe ignored

their protests and signed the Slave Act of 1793. (This law should not be confused with the Fugitive Slave Act passed the same year in the United States.) The act did not free those who were already slaves, but it outlawed the slave trade in Upper Canada, making sure no new slaves could be brought into the province. Upper Canada became the first British colony to pass a law against slavery.

Before the American Revolutionary War, Canada consisted of a large number of French-speaking citizens and small clusters of British settlers on the Atlantic Coast. With the great wave of Loyalists, the population of Canada began to grow rapidly. The settlers built new towns and opened up wilderness areas. New colonies had to be created to deal with the ever-growing numbers of people. The number of English speakers began to rival the French speakers, creating an interesting cultural mix.

At the same time as the eastern colonies grew and expanded, explorers and traders had begun to search out the unknown land to the west. The great fur trade that had sustained New France and created the Hudson's Bay Company was still in existence. By land, across the prairies, and by sea—around the tip of Africa or South America—the British rushed to discover what was on the other side of Canada.

The Canadian perspectives on slavery were influenced by the writings of Ignatius Sancho, a British intellectual and author.

Three
EXPLORING THE WEST

"Land, ho!" The cry went up at daybreak on March 7, 1778. Through the rain and mist, mountains could be seen in the distance, and, closer to shore, snow lay thick on the ground. *At last*, Captain James Cook thought, looking at the dreary landscape.

He and his crew had left Britain nearly two years earlier on their third trip around the world, this time looking for the Pacific Coast of North America. His purpose was to find the Northwest Passage—the fabled sea route leading through the continent and linking the Atlantic and Pacific. For centuries, explorers had searched the Atlantic coastline for an entrance to the passage; now, Cook would search the opposite side of North America.

The British Arrive on the West Coast

James Cook was not the first European to reach the west coast of North America. The Spanish, traveling north from Mexico, had claimed the entire coast several years earlier, and the Russians had been established in Alaska since the 1740s.

Cook was, however, the first British explorer to reach the Pacific Coast, arriving at the same time as Britain battled for control

Captain Cook

of its American colonies a continent away. Cook first glimpsed what is now Oregon on the morning of March 7, 1778, but since the weather was so unpleasant, he did not try to go ashore; instead, he continued to sail north. On March 29, Cook took his two ships, the *Resolution* and the *Discovery*, into an inlet and anchored them in the sheltered harbor they found there.

Cook had expected the area to be uninhabited, but to his surprise he saw a group of Natives on the shore. Soon, the Native people began bringing furs to the British to trade. Cook asked the people the name of their tribe, but they didn't understand him and thought he was asking for the best route around one of the islands. They told him to "come around," which was "Nootka" in their language. Cook reported in his journals that the name of the First Nations people he had encountered was the Nootka and named the area Nootka Sound.

The British stayed in Nootka Sound for nearly a month, repairing their ships and trading with the Natives. Then the British continued on their journey north to look for the Northwest Passage. During the summer and early fall, Cook tried several times to sail through the Bering Strait, but the ice and harsh weather kept turning him back. Finally, he gave up and sailed back to the Hawaiian Islands, where he was killed in a fight with the Hawaiians over a stolen boat.

Cook had discovered Vancouver Island, though he had not realized it was an island. He had passed the Strait of Juan de Fuca separating the southern end of the island from the mainland, but he had thought it was only a shallow harbor. Other explorers had seen the island as they sailed by, but

Cook was the first to land on it (in Nootka Sound on Vancouver Island's west coast).

West Coast Conflicts

When Cook's ships returned to Britain, the British were thrilled with the furs they had brought back, especially the beautiful, silky sea otter furs. The East Coast fur trade had focused on beaver pelts, but now people wanted sea otter. Over the next few years, British ships began to flow into the area, sailing away with their holds filled with sea otter pelts. Soon, the Nootka region had roused the interest of most of the world's colonial powers.

In 1788, John Meares, a British trader sailing under a Portuguese flag, arrived in Nootka Sound and claimed to have negotiated a trade agreement with the Nootka chief Maquinna—although Maquinna later denied any agreement and called Meares a liar. When Meares left to spend the winter in China, the Spanish arrived, having heard rumors that the Russians had begun to move in on their territory.

Spanish captain Esteban Martínez captured the ship Meares had left behind and started building a settlement. Spain had ordered him to construct a temporary fort, but he liked the area and wanted to see a more permanent presence established at Nootka. He put up buildings, planted gardens, and ordered a bell for the church he planned to construct.

In July, four British ships arrived, sent by Meares to begin building a fort. Martínez quickly captured the ships and sent them south to Mexico with the British as prisoners.

Chief Maquinna

When Meares heard the news in China, he left immediately to get help from Britain.

The British were indignant over the actions of the Spanish—which had been greatly exaggerated by Meares. Soon relations between Britain and Spain had deteriorated to the point where war threatened. Neither country really wanted a war. Neither could afford a war. In 1790, they hastily put together an agreement, the Nootka Convention of 1790. Under the terms of the convention, the Spanish would give Nootka Sound back to the British. The British would be allowed to trade along the Pacific Coast, but they could not go near Spanish forts.

To officially receive Nootka back from the Spanish, Britain sent Captain George Vancouver to North America's West Coast. Vancouver arrived in 1792 and met with the Spanish commander, Juan Francisco de la Bodega y Quadra, in Nootka Sound. By this time, Bodega y Quadra had determined that Meares had not established the extensive claims he maintained he had. The Spanish commander decided he would not give up the land, since he felt Meares did not have a legitimate claim. Neither Vancouver nor Bodega y Quadra were willing to compromise, and both continued to claim the land around Nootka Sound. Vancouver had been sent to take back the land and was not authorized to negotiate further. Finally, seeing they were getting nowhere, the two men agreed to send messages to Europe and let Britain and Spain decide what should be done.

Vancouver stayed on the West Coast for the next two years, waiting to hear the results of the Nootka negotiations. While he waited, he explored the coastline and made

Vancouver's discovery of Mount Rainier

George Vancouver

a detailed survey. He was the first to realize Nootka Sound lay on the coast of an island, not the mainland. He named the island Quadra and Vancouver's Island after himself and the Spanish commander.

Back in Europe, Britain and Spain first decided the two countries would share Nootka Sound as a neutral area, but in 1794, they signed the third Nootka Convention, agreeing to completely leave the area. Vancouver's survey had shown no possible outlet of the Northwest Passage, and neither nation had the time or money to devote to building permanent settlements without the benefit of a trade route.

Interior Fur Trade

While British sailors explored Canada's Pacific Coast, fur traders began to push

*A **monopoly** is a situation in which one company controls an industry or is the only provider of a product or service.*

Alexander Mackenzie

further and further inland from the east. When France had surrendered their Canadian colonies to the British in 1763, the British-run Hudson's Bay Company was left as the only major trading company in the area. The Hudson's Bay Company, however, had focused mainly on Hudson Bay and James Bay, choosing to let First Nations traders bring furs to their forts instead of sending men inland.

With the French trading companies gone, enterprising British merchants moved into Montréal and quickly hired French Canadian traders. These traders were familiar with the woods and rivers, and they had First Nations contacts. In the 1780s, the merchants came together to form the North West Company. Their aim was to break the northern **monopoly** of the Hudson's Bay Company and to take over the industry themselves. The North West Company had the money to finance inland exploration, opening up new trade routes and mapping out previously unknown rivers and lakes.

The Métis

French Canadian *coureurs de bois* and voyageurs—traders who lived in the wild, traveling the rivers in birch bark canoes—often married women from the First Nations tribes they encountered. The children born of these relationships became known as the Métis, meaning "mixed blood." The Métis, with their shared European and First Nations heritage, formed their own tribes. These groups often worked with fur traders and were hired by the North West Company.

The American troops were frightened of the First Nations warriors.

fort at Detroit. Then, Brock and Tecumseh planned an attack on Detroit itself.

General Hull and his men feared the First Nations warriors. The more they saw Tecumseh and his men outside their fort, the more frightened they became. Brock used this fear to his advantage. When he sent a letter requesting Hull's surrender, he casually mentioned that he was afraid he would not be able to restrain the Native warriors in an attack. Although Tecumseh had only six hundred men with him, these warriors whooped and shouted outside Fort Detroit, making the Americans inside believe they were completely overrun. Brock encouraged this impression by allowing Hull to capture a false message in which he requested five thousand more warriors. When Brock finally attacked the fort on August 16, Hull immediately surrendered.

*A **militia** is a fighting force of civilian soldiers who have taken military training and who serve as full-time soldiers during emergencies.*

The Battle of Detroit was a huge British victory, showing the Americans that Canada would not be as easily captured as they had assumed. Brock's decisive actions and the help of Tecumseh also encouraged the Canadians. Both Brock and Tecumseh would be killed in battle during the war, Brock at the Battle of Queenston Heights in November 1812—where the British successfully pushed back another American invasion—and Tecumseh a year later at the Battle of the Thames, an American victory. Although the war would last for another two years after the capture of Detroit, Canada was never truly in danger of falling to the Americans.

The Battle of York

One of the few major American victories on Canadian soil came in April of 1813.

Laura Secord

Laura Secord is known as a Canadian heroine. She, her husband, and their five children lived at Queenston in Upper Canada. When her husband was wounded in the Battle of Queenston Heights, Laura searched the battlefield until she found him and brought him home. In 1813, the Americans invaded again and demanded the Secords house several American officers. Laura overheard the Americans talking about a surprise attack they were planning and set off to warn the British. She walked nearly twenty miles (32 kilometers), part of it barefoot, until a group of Mohawk found her and took her to the British commanding officer. Although the British were hugely outnumbered in the following Battle of Beaver Dams, Laura's warning gave the British the information they needed to bluff the Americans into surrendering.

Laura Secord

declared Upper Canada captured, but American forces left York after only five days.

Americans Attack Lower Canada

Although most of the war was focused on the sparsely populated Upper Canada, in

American forces, led by General Zebulon Pike, sailed across Lake Ontario and landed at York—now Toronto—the little capital of Upper Canada. The British, under General Roger Sheaffe, were completely outnumbered. Sheaffe quickly realized there was no way he could win the battle. Just before pulling back, he set fire to the new warship being built in the harbor and lit fuses leading to the gunpowder storehouse. Many Americans, including General Pike, died in the explosion.

Although the Americans won the battle, capturing York and proceeding to loot and burn houses, they had lost more than they had won. Hundreds of men had died, and the American forces had not captured much of value. American General Henry Dearborn

General de Salaberry

45

Canadian men from sixteen to sixty years of age were required to serve in the militia that fought off American attacks.

late 1813 the Americans launched two separate attacks on Lower Canada. The first attack came north through Lake Champlain and up the Chateauguay River. The American general, Wade Hampton, knew very little about the forces he would face, while the Canadian commanding officer, Charles de Salaberry, had gathered detailed information about the approaching Americans. In this battle, the Americans faced Canadian troops fighting without the aid of the British Army.

General Hampton and his four thousand men mistakenly believed the Canadians outnumbered his forces. In reality, de Salaberry waited with about only five hundred Canadians and Mohawks. As the British and Canadians had done in past battles of the war, de Salaberry used the American fear of Native warriors to intimidate the invaders. He blew horns and sent the Mohawks through the woods shouting war cries, convincing Hampton he was facing a huge force. When the Americans reached a barricade in the road, the Canadians attacked. The strength of the attack, along with the American belief that they faced only a fraction of the defenders, panicked Hampton's men. They retreated, never knowing they outnumbered their enemy eight to one.

The second American attack in Lower Canada came from the west, along the St. Lawrence River, heading for Montréal. Again the Americans outnumbered the defenders, this time nearly ten to one. The British, however, were a well-trained force, used to battles from the wars in Europe. The Americans were a ragtag group, their attacks chaotic and clumsy. The British, with the aid of the Canadian militia and First Nations fighters, easily blocked the

The War in the East

The New England states did not support the War of 1812. They had close trade ties with New Brunswick and Nova Scotia and did not care about conquering Canada. In fact, when the United States forbade trade with the British North American colonies, many in New England ignored the law and started a booming smuggling business. The New Englanders were so against the war they threatened to separate from the rest of the United States.

American advances until the attackers gave up and retreated.

The British Invade the United States

The United States had declared war on Britain at a time when the British were distracted by wars in France against the emperor Napoleon Bonaparte. In April of 1814, however, a European alliance defeated Napoleon and exiled him to an island in the Mediterranean. After this, the British had more resources available for fighting in North America. To avenge the American capture and destruction of their Canadian capital at York, the British launched a major attack against the Washington, D.C., area.

In August of 1814, the British arrived in Maryland and began marching toward the American capital. The Americans had gathered a force of nearly seven thousand to face the 4,500 British soldiers. The president, James Madison, rode out with several of his cabinet members to watch the battle, although the secretary of war had warned him it might be a bad idea.

The poorly trained Americans were not prepared to deal with the British regulars, who had just come from years of war in Europe. The line of defenders wavered and

The British attack on Washington

then broke. Soon people were running wildly up the streets, retreating in panic as the British moved toward Washington. Along with many government members and politicians, President Madison was caught up in the rush and fled to safety. First Lady Dolly Madison stayed at the White House long after most had retreated to safety. She gathered pictures and documents, packing them up to carry them away, until she was finally persuaded to leave just before the arrival of the British.

The British found Washington virtually undefended when they entered the city. They proceeded to burn and loot, as the

Americans had done at York. They rampaged through the White House, leaving it damaged and scorched. Later, the president's home would be quickly whitewashed to cover the burn marks, leading to its name: the White House.

From Washington, the British proceeded toward Baltimore, an important military target. Baltimore was heavily fortified, with sixteen thousand American troops and supplies to last an extended siege. The British attacked with only five thousand men and were easily defeated, although the battle

A painting represents the peace brought by the Treaty of Ghent.

raged for three days. The British retreated from the area to prepare for another attack elsewhere.

On December 24, 1814, representatives from the United States and Great Britain signed the Treaty of Ghent, ending the War of 1812. The Americans had been trying to end the war almost since they had started it. They had quickly realized conquering Canada would not be the "mere matter of marching" they had hoped.

The war ended in a stalemate; no one won. The real losers in the war, though, were the First Nations. They had joined the British, fighting to keep American settlers off their land. They believed they would receive permanent land in return for their help. Instead, they were ignored. The treaty said they would receive "all the possessions, rights, and privileges" they had before the war, but this promise was vague and easily avoided by settlers moving west.

One thing the war had accomplished for Canada was that it reinforced its differences from the United States. This helped to build a sense of Canadian identity. Several years later, however, Canada would face its own internal crisis. In a land where two distinct nations—French and English—lived side by side, a growing dissatisfaction and desire for self-rule would soon bring about rebellions and uprisings.

French fur traders and the First Nations often worked together, but their rivalry with the British led to tension.

Five
GROWING PAINS

Cuthbert Grant wanted to avoid Fort Douglas at all cost. The Hudson's Bay Company colony at the fort had issued the *Pemmican* Proclamation two years earlier, after several hard winters, forbidding anyone to transport food out of Assiniboia, the Red River Colony. This meant the Métis—descendants of French Canadian and First Nations intermarriages—could not transport pemmican to their allies in the North West Company.

Grant and the other Métis did not believe the Hudson's Bay Company had any right to tell them what to do, but they avoided the fort just the same. They had avoided the fort many times in the past, but this time they were spotted.

Before long, Grant heard the thunder of hooves as Governor Semple and a group of settlers galloped up behind them. Grant motioned for his men to spread out around a cluster of trees known as Seven Oaks. Someone fired a shot, and suddenly chaos broke out. When the dust cleared, Governor Semple and twenty of his men lay dead. Only two Métis had been killed.

Pemmican is a traditional Native food made with strips of dried meat pounded into a paste and then mixed with melted fat, dried berries or fruits, and pressed into little cakes.

Fur-Trade Rivals

The Pemmican Wars were a result of the bitter rivalry between the Hudson's Bay Company and the North West Company. The Hudson's Bay Company had formed in 1670, but for the first hundred years of its existence it had kept to the shores of Hudson Bay and James Bay. The North West Company, established in 1783, had aggressively struck out into the interior of Canada, sending explorers all the way to the Pacific Ocean by 1793. In response, the Hudson's Bay Company had also moved inland.

The Beothuk

In some parts of Canada, First Nations people formed alliances with European colonists, but in Newfoundland, the Beothuk people stayed away from the white settlers. Before the arrival of Europeans, the Beothuk had lived along the coasts, but as fishing communities grew up in the harbors and coves, the Beothuk retreated inland. Food was scarce in the interior of Newfoundland, and many Beothuk died of starvation. When white trappers moved inland, the Beothuk stole from them, and in turn, the trappers slaughtered any Beothuk they found. In 1823, fur traders captured three Beothuk women. Two died almost immediately, but one, Shawnandithit, lived for another six years in captivity. She drew pictures of the Beothuk lifestyle and culture, describing as much as she could before she died of tuberculosis. Although explorers searched for the Beothuk after this, no more were found. The arrival of the white man had led to the extinction of the Beothuk.

In 1812, Lord Selkirk, under the protection of the Hudson's Bay Company, had built a colony in the Red River Valley, at what is now Winnipeg, Manitoba. The new colony, Fort Douglas, was located deep in the territory of the North West Company. In 1815, the Nor'westerns—men from the North West Company—attacked the fort and drove the settlers away, but the settlers returned and rebuilt.

On June 19, 1816, a small group of Métis, led by Cuthbert Grant, exchanged gunfire with settlers from Fort Douglas. The Hudson's Bay Company considered the encounter a massacre, since almost all the settlers had been killed. For the Métis,

A Beothuk dwelling

however, the Battle of Seven Oaks quickly became known as the moment when they became a nation.

In retaliation for the death of Governor Semple and his men, the Hudson's Bay Company sent troops to the area and captured a North West Company fort. The hostilities might have continued for years, but the British government stepped in and ordered both companies to stop fighting and make peace. With the continued government pressure, the companies finally agreed to merge in July of 1821. Suddenly, the Hudson's Bay Company had a monopoly on the entire Canadian fur trade.

The Rebellions of 1837

When the Constitutional Act of 1791 had created the separate colonies of Upper and Lower Canada, the government had been laid out to make sure the people were not given too much freedom. The American Revolutionary War had been over for less than ten years, and the British were nervous about allowing colonists too much say in how they were governed. Too much freedom, they thought, had led the American colonies to revolt. Upper and Lower Canada were therefore ruled by an appointed governor, a council appointed by the governor, and an assembly elected by the people. The

The Rebellion of 1837

Cliques are small groups of friends or colleagues who have similar interests and goals, and who are seen as exclusive by outsiders.

Someone who is **liberal** is broadminded and tolerant of different views and standards of behavior.

Louis-Joseph Papineau

assembly ensured the people had some say in their own governing, but the assembly could do nothing without the approval of both the governor and the council.

The government structure in Canada enabled the rise of several powerful *cliques* made up of wealthy men who gave out council positions to their friends. In Lower Canada, the Chateau Clique ruled; in Upper Canada, the Family Compact controlled the government. Anyone not favored by the ruling powers could do little to change society, even if supported by most Canadians. In Lower Canada, the French were almost entirely shut out of the council, even though they outnumbered the English.

Canadians wanted a more democratic system. They wanted to be able to have an input in government decisions. They became increasingly frustrated with their lack of power, but as long as the Chateau Clique and the Family Compact were in power, they could do nothing.

In Lower Canada, the *parti patriote*, led by Louis-Joseph Papineau, formed to counteract the Chateau Clique. The parti patriote was made up of **liberal** French Canadians opposed to what they saw as a corrupt and evil government. The group became popular in Lower Canada, and parti patriote members held most of the elected assembly seats. In 1834, they drew up a list called the 92 Resolutions, which outlined their complaints against the current government. They wanted a reform of the existing system, giving the elected assembly control of the colony's funds and also making the governor choose the appointed council from elected assembly members.

The British government took years to respond to the 92 Resolutions, but when they finally did, in 1837, they rejected them completely. The parti patriote was enraged. Papineau

Montgomery's Tavern

gave angry speeches, and the crowds cheered him, roaring for change. Dr. Wolfred Nelson, an English Canadian, joined the group and started calling for revolution. At that point, Papineau began to back down. He wanted change, but he did not want to lead a war.

Led by Nelson, an untrained group of rebels fought British troops at St-Denis on November 23, 1837, and won. Two days later, the British returned and put down the rebellion, killing sixty and capturing many more. On December 14, the British crushed another outbreak of rebellion at St-Eustache, near Montréal.

In Upper Canada, a separate rebellion had been brewing, stirred up by much the same complaints as in Lower Canada, with the Family Compact in place of the Chateau Clique. Newspaper publisher William Lyon

*To show **favoritism** is to show preference for one thing or person over another.*

***Radicals** are people who favor major changes.*

*To be **assimilated** is to be integrated into a larger group so that differences are minimized.*

John George Lambton

Mackenzie led the movement. Like the parti patriote in Lower Canada, he too gathered a list of complaints to send to Great Britain. The Upper Canada document was called the Report on Grievances and included many objections to the current government. Apart from the desire for a more democratic government, a major complaint was the *favoritism* shown the Anglican Church, while other Protestant churches were given few rights.

When the Lower Canada Rebellion began in 1837, the *radicals* in Upper Canada made their move. The governor of Upper Canada, Francis Bond Head, sent troops from Toronto to help put down the eastern rebellion, and Mackenzie and his supporters traveled to the city to lead an uprising. On December 4, more than six hundred angry Canadians met at Montgomery's Tavern on Yonge Street north of Toronto. The rebels, armed with guns and pitchforks, poured into the street and began a march toward the city. A small group of militia, all the troops left in the city, turned out to fight the men from Montgomery's Tavern. The militia fired, and the rebels fled almost immediately.

Neither the Lower nor Upper Canada rebellion was successful. Most of the radical leaders escaped to the United States. Those who did not were arrested, and some were executed the following year. Louis-Joseph Papineau, Wolfred Nelson, and William Lyon Mackenzie were all pardoned in the 1840s and returned to Canada.

Act of Union

Although the rebellions of 1837 might appear to have accomplished nothing—and it must have seemed that way to their

Louis-Hippolyte LaFontaine

ous year. Lord Durham toured Lower and Upper Canada, and the following year he released his report.

Durham recommended the colonies be allowed to govern themselves, except on certain matters. He found the system of ruling cliques was largely to blame for the unrest and advised that the governor should take his council from the elected assembly members (as the radicals wanted). He also believed that the existence of both French and English Canadians had caused many of the problems in Lower Canada. He urged that the French be *assimilated* into the English population as much as possible. To make this easier, he proposed uniting Upper and Lower Canada into one colony, ruled by one governor. In this way, the English would be in the majority. The new colony would be ruled strictly by British laws, and English would be the only official language. He believed the French would then gradually be absorbed into the English culture.

In 1841, a year after Lord Durham died, Britain passed the Act of Union. Under the Act, Upper and Lower Canada would be united into one colony, with the two parts known as Canada West and Canada East. Britain adopted some, but not all, of Durham's recommendations. Specifically, the existing appointed council and elected assembly system was kept, meaning

leaders in the years afterward—they actually had a huge impact on the growth of Canada. The British were certainly now aware of the dissatisfaction of the Canadian people.

In 1838, John George Lambton, earl of Durham, arrived in Canada, sent by the British government to look into the conditions leading to the rebellions of the previ-

Canadians still would have little say in their own government. Although Durham had suggested electing a number of representatives from Canada West and East based on population, the Act of Union allowed for an equal number from each section. The French-speaking Canada East had the greater population, and Britain wanted to make sure the French could not gain a majority in the assembly.

Despite the attempts of the British to make sure the French were assimilated into English Canadian culture, *moderate* reformers within the government were able to pass several laws ensuring the continuation of the French language and culture. An education act gave Canada West a public school system, while allowing for religious schools in Canada East, most of which would be French Catholic. In 1848, part of the Act of Union was *amended* to include French as an official language of Canada.

Finally, later that same year, the Act of Union was amended again to allow the province of Canada to govern itself. Robert Baldwin and Louis-Hippolyte LaFontaine, reformers from Canada West and Canada East, led the way to a new government. Britain had recently passed new laws concerning its colonies, so when the governor, Lord Elgin, saw the people had overwhelmingly elected the two reformers to the assembly, he asked them to form a new government. Lord Elgin stepped down as governor and moved to the symbolic position of governor general. Canada had won the fight for self-government, the first step in becoming an independent country.

Oregon Country

On the Pacific Coast, Hudson's Bay Company fur traders did business with First Nations people, while American settlers spread west across the plains. The border between Canada and the United States had been drawn along the forty-ninth parallel from the Great Lakes to the Rockies, but the land beyond the Rocky Mountains—Oregon Country—was occupied by both Britain and the United States. Oregon Country stretched from Alaska in the north to California in the south.

Manifest Destiny, the idea that God meant the American people to occupy the entire continent of North America,

*Someone who is a **moderate** is middle-of-the-road, not extreme, in his or her beliefs or actions.*

*Legislation that has been **amended** has been formally altered or revised.*

The border between the United States and Canada dipped south around Vancouver Island.

became a rallying cry in the United States. Americans believed that the number of their settlers moving into the West should stake their claim on Oregon Country.

The Hudson's Bay Company realized the ownership of Oregon Country would soon need to be decided. In the early 1840s, the company sent James Douglas to build a trading fort on Vancouver Island. Such a fort would be a mark of ownership for the British. Douglas searched the island for the perfect spot to build the new fort. In 1843, he

British Columbia

Six

CONFEDERATION: CANADA BECOMES A NATION

To the south, the United States was in turmoil. Southern slave owners clashed with Northern *abolitionists*. As new states joined the country, politicians struggled to keep the number of slave and free states equal. With growing concern, Canadians watched the division in their southern neighbor.

In 1861, a bloody civil war erupted between the Northern Union states and the Southern Confederate states who had tried to break away and form their own country. Americans in the North thought the Canadians should help them fight. Although a few individual Canadians crossed the border to join the American Army, Britain—and therefore Canada—remained officially neutral.

Many Americans, annoyed by the lack of Canadian support, again wanted to take over the land to their north and get rid of the British in North America. As soon as they had dealt with those rebel Southerners, Northern journalists wrote, they would tackle the problem of British North America.

Abolitionists were people who campaigned against slavery during the eighteenth and nineteenth centuries.

Union soldiers sang to the tune of "Yankee Doodle" as they marched,

Secession first he would put down
Wholly and forever,
And afterwards from Britain's crown
He Canada would sever.

The Deadlock

In the 1850s, the province of Canada was governed by two men: John A. Macdonald in Canada West and George-Étienne Cartier in Canada East. Macdonald and Cartier were both lawyers and conservatives. They believed in the British monarchy and in keeping most of the power in the hands of the government. Their main political opponents were the Liberals, led by George Brown of the Reform Party in Canada West and by Antoine-Aimé Dorion of the *parti rouge* in Canada East.

For the English Canadians in Canada West, representation by population became an increasingly heated issue. When Upper and Lower Canada had been combined into one province in 1841, each half of the province had been given an equal number of representatives rather than a number based on population. At the time, the British

John A. Macdonald

had believed this would underrepresent the French Canadians, who had the greater population. Since then, the number of English Canadians had grown, and by 1861, the population of Canada West was much greater than that of Canada East. Now, the English Canadians were the ones being underrepresented.

While Canadians in Canada West wanted to change the system to include representa-

The divisions between Canada West, English-speaking and Protestant, and Canada East, French-speaking and Roman Catholic, increased to the point where very little could be accomplished because the assembly was deadlocked. Added to this division were the quarrels between the Conservatives and the Liberals.

Something needed to be done to solve the problems in the Canadian political system.

George-Étienne Cartier

CONFEDERATION!

A political cartoon portrays the "fathers" of confederation, including Macdonald, Cartier, and Brown.

tion by population, those in Canada East did not. If the system were changed, they would have fewer representatives than the other half of Canada. The debate ground to a standstill, with politicians from Canada West and Canada East on different sides of the issue.

The United States was being torn apart by civil war, and at the same time, threatening to take over Canada. The Canadians needed a strong government to deal with the threat of invasion. In 1864, George Brown of the Liberals agreed to join the Conservatives in order to break the deadlock. Brown promised to add his support to Macdonald and Cartier if together they would work to create a confederation of provinces in British North America. Under this confederation, Canada West and Canada East would each become a separate province again, represented in a central federal government according to population. The Great Coalition, as the partnership of Macdonald, Cartier, and Brown was called, would also work to bring the Atlantic Provinces into the plan and to extend the confederacy into the West.

The Conference at Charlottetown

While the Great Coalition in the province of Canada discussed how best to create a confederacy of Canadian provinces, New Brunswick, Nova Scotia, and Prince Edward Island had already begun to discuss uniting to better deal with the threat of invasion from the United States. They planned to

meet in Charlottetown, Prince Edward Island, to talk about the details of the proposed union. When the Canadians heard about these talks, they asked if they could attend the conference as well, to discuss creating a confederacy of the entire British North America.

On September 1, 1864, delegates from Canada West, Canada East, New Brunswick, Nova Scotia, and Prince Edward Island met at Charlottetown. At the last minute, Newfoundland was invited to attend, but they did not send any delegates.

The conference lasted nearly a week, and by the end, the delegates were enthusiastic about uniting their provinces into a confederacy. They went home, agreeing to meet again in Québec City the next month.

The Conference at Québec City

Beginning on October 10, the two-week conference at Québec City dealt with the structure of the new confederacy. Delegates from all the eastern provinces, including Newfoundland, joined the talks. Macdonald wanted one strong single government to

The Charlottetown Conference

rule the union, but most of the delegates objected. British North America was so large many felt one government could not adequately represent the interests of all the provinces. French Canadians also worried about protecting the French language and culture.

Macdonald believed the American Civil War was caused by giving the individual states too much freedom. He wanted to make sure a similar problem never happened in British North America. For this reason, he felt the new confederacy needed a strong federal government.

Finally, the delegates compromised. They would have a blended system, with a federal government and provincial governments. Each government would have different responsibilities, and the federal government would assume any responsibilities not specifically mentioned.

The new country would be called the Dominion of Canada, and it would not be completely independent from Great Britain. Foreign affairs would still be dealt with by Britain, and Queen Victoria would appoint a governor general to oversee affairs in Canada.

Federal vs. Provincial

Under the government of the new country, the federal and provincial governments would have different responsibilities.

Federal:
defense, criminal law, First Nations concerns, currency, banking, navigation and shipping, marriage and divorce, and the fisheries

Provincial:
civil law, natural resources, education, roads, cities and towns, and medicine

Canada after confederation

Macdonald, Cartier, and some of the other Conservative politicians were still worried about giving the people too much freedom. To balance the voice of the people, the new government would have both a Senate and a House of Commons. The members of Parliament in the House of Commons would be elected, with each province represented based on population. The smaller provinces would only have a few members representing them in the House of Commons, while Canada East and Canada West would receive 75 percent of the members. The senators, however, would be appointed for life, with a certain number of senators for each region.

Gaining Support

Finally, having drawn up what they called the Québec Resolutions, or the 72 Resolutions, the delegates went back to convince their home provinces to agree to the proposed confederation. All the delegates had signed the resolutions, but each province still needed to agree to join the Confederation.

The province of Canada had no trouble gaining support for the proposed confederation, but the others had a much more difficult time. Many people in the Atlantic provinces thought they would be better off forming their own union, separate from Canada. Canada East and Canada West, with the majority of Members of Parliament in the House of Commons, would be pretty much in control of the new country. Prince Edward Island, who would have only 6 of 194 members of Parliament, and Newfoundland, who would have 8, both rejected confederation. After a long battle, Nova Scotia and New Brunswick agreed to join. All that was left was to present the plan to Britain.

Fenian Invasion

The United States had often threatened to take over British North America, invading during both the Revolutionary War and the War of 1812. During the Civil War, Americans in the Northern states again began to talk of capturing Canada. In 1866, an annexation bill was introduced in the U.S. House of Representatives. The bill was titled "A Bill for the admission of the States of Nova Scotia, New Brunswick, Canada East, and Canada West, and for the organization of the Territories of Selkirk, Saskatchewan, and Columbia." The bill never made it into law, but the sentiment, echoed again and again in the United States, made the Canadians uneasy.

In 1866, after the American Civil War had ended, a group of Fenians started

Canada's Parliament buildings today

making border raids into Canada. The Fenians were Irish Americans who wanted to free Ireland from British rule (the name came from the legendary Gaelic hero Finn MacCool). They believed that by threatening Canada they would put pressure on Britain—in a way using Canada as a hostage to try and force Great Britain to do what they wanted.

The United States did not officially support the Fenians, but they did not go out of their way to prevent them from invading Canada. After all, the United States had been talking about conquering British North America for years.

The Fenians had been able to gather large amounts of weapons for their attacks—

Modern-day sign marking the site of the Fenian invasion

Political cartoon portraying the Fenians

surplus left from the war—and they had found many bored young men who were willing to fight with them. They did not think the Canadians would be too difficult to defeat.

The Fenians had been overconfident. The Canadians heard news of their coming and were able to gather troops to meet them. After a series of unsuccessful attacks, the Fenians were scattered and many arrested.

The people of British North America had been alarmed by the raids, but they had also gained confidence by the way their own forces had been able to defeat the invaders. They realized that the provinces would be stronger in a confederacy than on their own; jointly, they would be able to turn away even larger attacks. The most important outcome of the Fenian raids was the push they gave many—especially in New Brunswick—to support confederation.

Confederation

During the winter of 1866 and 1867, the confederation delegates met again, this time in London, England. Britain was ready to grant its North American colonies a greater measure of freedom. Defense against the threat of the United States had gotten expensive, and Britain was willing to let the provinces of British North America come together to take care of the issue themselves. Britain would

The confederation meeting in London

still keep some control over the new country of Canada, but with much less involvement.

In the spring of 1867, Queen Victoria signed the British North America Act, uniting the province of Canada—now to be known as Quebec and Ontario—New Brunswick, and Nova Scotia into the Dominion of Canada. Part of the British North America Act stated that a railway linking the provinces had to be built from the St. Lawrence River to Halifax, Nova Scotia. On July 1, 1867, the act went into effect. Canada was now a country.

In the hundred years before confederation, British North America had gone from an established French Canadian population in the St. Lawrence region and a few small English settlements to the Dominion of Canada, to a country of four provinces and a population of three and a half million. Canada had survived American invasions during the Revolutionary War and the War of 1812. It had come through internal turmoil during the Rebellions of 1837. Explorers had pushed west to reach the Pacific and the new colony of British Columbia had been founded.

In the years after confederation, the new country would continue to grow, adding new provinces and expanding to the west and north.

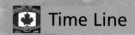
October 7, 1763 King George issues the Royal Proclamation of 1763, forbidding settlement west of the Appalachian Mountains.

September 1775 America launches an attack against Québec.

1670 The Hudson's Bay Company is formed.

1775 The American colonists hold the Second Continental Congress and invite the Canadians to send delegates.

December 31, 1775 Americans attack Québec City and lose decisively.

1790 Britain and Spain sign the Nootka Convention of 1790, agreeing to share the area.

1763 The British conquer Québec.

1774 Britain passes the Quebec Act.

1784 Nova Scotia is divided into three colonies. (In 1820, Cape Breton Island rejoins Nova Scotia.)

1791 The Constitutional Act splits the province of Québec into two parts—Upper Canada and Lower Canada.

July 12, 1812 General William Hull crosses the Canadian border from Detroit and offers friendship to Canadians, as long as they did not fight on the side of the British.

1792 Approximately 1,200 Black Loyalists leave Nova Scotia and travel to Africa, where they found Sierra Leone.

June 18, 1812 The United States declares war on Britain and begins to work on invading Canada.

1794 Britain and Spain sign the third Nootka Convention, agreeing to leave the area completely.

August 16, 1812 General William Hull surrenders to the British at the Battle of Detroit.

1793 John Graves Simcoe begins to build the new capital of Upper Canada at York (now Toronto).

July 1793 Alexander Mackenzie of the North West Company reaches the Pacific Ocean.

December 24, 1814 Representatives from the United States and Great Britain sign the Treaty of Ghent, ending the War of 1812.

1841 Britain passes the Act of Union, joining Upper and Lower Canada.

April 1813 Americans defeat the British at the Battle of York.

1834 The parti patriote draws up the 92 Resolutions; the British government rejects them three years later.

1837 The Lower Canada Rebellion begins.

1848 The Act of Union is amended to include French as an official language of Canada and to grant the province of Canada the right to govern itself.

July 1821 The Hudson's Bay Company and the North West Company are forced to merge by the British government.

1849 Vancouver Island becomes a British colony, the first west of the Great Lakes.

August 1814 The British arrive in Maryland and begin marching toward Washington, D.C.

1864 British Columbia is granted self-rule.

1866 Vancouver Island and British Columbia merge into a single colony under the name British Columbia.

1857 Gold is found along the Fraser River in British Columbia.

Spring 1867 Queen Victoria signs the British North America Act, creating the Dominion of Canada.

August 2, 1858 Britain creates the colony of British Columbia.

July 1, 1867 The British North America Act goes into effect, and Canada becomes a country.

October 10, 1864 Delegates from all eastern provinces meet to form the structure of the new confederacy.

1866 "A Bill for the admission of the States of Nova Scotia, New Brunswick, Canada East, and Canada West, and for the organization of the Territories of Selkirk, Saskatchewan, and Columbia" is introduced in the U.S. House of Representatives.

FURTHER READING

Beckett, Harry. *Nova Scotia*. Vero Beach, Fla.: Rourke Publishing, 1997.

Bliss, Michael. *Confederation: A New Nationality*. Toronto: Grolier Limited, 1981.

Ferry, Steven. *Ontario*. San Diego, Calif.: Lucent Books, 2003.

Gann, Marjorie. *New Brunswick*. New York: Scholastic Library Publishing, 1997.

Greenblatt, Miriam. *War of 1812*. New York: Facts on File, 2003. Toronto: Kids Can Press, 2002.

Mackay, Claire. *Toronto Story*. Toronto: Annick Press, 2002.

Nanton, Isabel, Nancy Flight, and Barbara Tomlin. *British Columbia*. New York: Scholastic Library Publishing, 1994.

Provencer, Jean. *Quebec*. New York: Scholastic Library Publishing, 1992.

Smolinski, Diane, and Henry Smolinski. *Battles of the War of 1812*. Chicago, Ill.: Heinemann Library, 2002.

Turner, Wesley. *Life in Upper Canada*. Toronto: Grolier Limited, 1980.

FOR MORE INFORMATION

The Battle of Quebec
theamericanrevolution.org/battles/
bat_queb.asp

The Battle of Seven Oaks
www.metisresourcecentre.mb.ca/history/
oaks.htm

The Black Loyalists
collections.ic.gc.ca/blackloyalists/
wireframe.htm

Canadian Confederation
www.collectionscanada.ca/confederation/
index-e.html

Fraser River Gold Rush
www.fortlangley.ca/langley/2arush.html

Hudson's Bay Company History
www.hbc.com/hbcheritage/

The Métis Nation
www.metisnation.ca/ARTS/hist_who.html

Nova Scotia During the American
Revolution
odur.let.rug.nl/~usa/E/novascotia/
scotiaxx.htm

Pathfinders and Passageways, The
Exploration of Canada: Exploring
Westward
www.collectionscanada.ca/explorers/
h24-1500-e.html

Pathfinders and Passageways, The
Exploration of Canada: The Pacific Coast
www.collectionscanada.ca/explorers/
h24-1700-e.html

The War of 1812
www.multied.com/1812/Index.html

INDEX

PICTURE CREDITS

Canada Parks: pp. 45 (right), 46

Dover: pp. 65, 66–67

Library of Congress: pp. 14, 38–39, 48, 49

National Archives of Canada: pp. 1, 8–9, 10–11, 22–23, 24–25, 26–27, 28, 56, 59, 68, 69 (right), 70–71, 77, 78–79

National Gallery of Ontario: p. 29

National Library of Canada: p. 73

Photos.com: pp. 13, 60–61, 62–63, 74–75

Provincial Archives of Newfoundland and Labrador: p. 53

Trent University: p. 12

U.S. National Archives and Records Administration: pp. 17, 18, 19

BIOGRAPHIES

Sheila Nelson was born in Newfoundland. She has written a number of history books for kids and always enjoys the chance to keep learning. She recently earned a master's degree and now lives in Rochester, New York, with her husband and daughter.

SERIES CONSULTANT

Dr. David Bercuson is the Director of the Centre for Military and Strategic Studies at the University of Calgary. His writings on modern Canadian politics, Canadian defense and foreign policy, and Canadian military, among other topics, have appeared in academic and popular publications. Dr. Bercuson is the author, coauthor, or editor of more than thirty books, including *Confrontation at Winnipeg: Labour, Industrial Relations, and the General Strike* (1990), *Colonies: Canada to 1867* (1992), *Maple Leaf Against the Axis, Canada's Second World War* (1995), and *Christmas in Washington: Roosevelt and Churchill Forge the Alliance* (2005). He has also served as historical consultant for several film and television projects, and provided political commentary for CBC radio and television and CTV television. In 1989, Dr. Bercuson was elected a fellow of the Royal Society of Canada. In 2004, Dr. Bercuson received the Vimy Award, sponsored by the Conference of Defence Association Institute, in recognition of his significant contributions to Canada's defense and the preservation of the Canadian democratic principles.